DAD'S ARMY SKETCHES

NICO BROEKHUIS

THE DUTCH DRAWER

City Stone Publishing

ISBN: 978-1-915399-17-5 (paperback)
ISBN: 978-1-915399-18-2 (e-PUB)

A CIP catalogue record for this book is available from the BritishLibrary.

Nico Broekhuis - The Dutch Drawer

City Stone Publishing - www.citystonepublishing.com

February 2023

SPECIAL THANKS

Dad's Army quotes and catchphrases by kind permission of Worldwide Theatrix Ltd (WWT Ltd) and Jimmy Perry Productions Ltd (JPP Ltd).

Drawings based on original pictures, scenes from Dad's Army by kind permission of the BBC.
© Drawings: Nico Broekhuis, the Netherlands
© Dad's Army quotes & catchphrases: WWT Ltd and JPP Ltd

WITH THIS BOOK, YOU SUPPORT THE ISLE OF WIGHT DONKEY SANCTUARY
A PERCENTAGE OF THE ROYALTIES GO TO THEIR CHARITY, NUMBER 1159886

Nico
2022

 FOREWORD

When Nico Broekhuis invited me to write a foreword for his book, I must admit, I didn't accept without hesitation I love *Dad's Army* and I watched every episode since it was first originally broadcasted.

Writing a foreword in a sketchbook by someone who calls himself a 'Dutch Drawer'? That seemed to me rather double Dutch. Being a history graduate, I accepted the invitation, in order to keep this Dutch Drawer under observation, only of course, in the best interest of the Dad's Army history and culture.

This book surprised me. You will find 59 Dad's Army drawings with the original quotes or catchphrases. Almost as if this Dutch Drawer was actually there, on the set, when he made his drawings.

Dad's Army is alive for over 50 years, not only in the English-speaking world but also in the Netherlands. I hope this work will put a smile on your face. I certainly smiled and nodded, recognising the characters on each page. A Dutch Drawer, paying a tribute to the culture and history of our beloved sitcom, *Dad's Army*, who would have thought that...

A not-so-famous historian, somewhere in England

DRAWINGS – INDEX

1.   SIR WINSTON CHURCHILL
2.   EL LAWRENCE
3.   YOUR FAVOURITE TOBACCO
4.   CARROTS AND ONIONS
5.   A FAG IN YOUR FOOD
6.   THE VERGER
7.   THE VICAR
8.   A LOT OF LAUGHING
9.   VIOLET GIBBONS
10. MRS PROSSER
11. PUT THAT LIGHT OUT
12. ACTUALLY, IT'S BLUE
13. OLD TRICKS AGAIN
14. FUNNY TEMPERED
15. GENERALE MONTEVERDI
16. ESSENTIAL SUPPLIES
17. NOT GIVING IN
18. A LAAAARGE BUILDING
19. NAPOLEON
20. MRS YEATMAN
21. THROUGH THE CEILING
22. A PRETTY BROOCH
23. SPECIAL DUTIES
24. MAD, MAD, MAD
25. THEM GERMANS MAKE...
26. IN A HUDDLE, AT THE DOUBLE
27. YOU WILL EAT SOGGY CHIPS
28. ON ZE LIST
29. DAVID COPPERFIELD
30. THE COLONEL
31. WHAT AM I?

32.   I HATE COWARDS
33.   OUTSTANDINGLY SUITABLE
34.   HONOUR YOUR WORKERS
35.   PWINCE 439
36.   GREAT SCOTT, GRAPES
37.   THE POWER OF THE PRESS
38.   HEAVILY DISGUISED
39.   MES CHERS CAMARADES
40.   NO KISS FOR THE VICAR
41.   IT'S WEDNESDAY
42.   IT MADE MEN OF US
43.   I COULDN'T DO HIM, DEAR
44.   CIS INSISTS...
45.   SCHWEINHUND...
46.   YOU LOOK LIKE AN EAGLE
47.   NICE BIT OF WEATHER...
48.   GOOD MORNING, MEIN HOST
49.   ALL BOYS DO IT, YOU KNOW
50.   NOT MY FRANK
51.   HAPPY LAUGHING FACES
52.   MERELY THE SERVANT
53.   YOUR COLLEAGUE?
54.   I'M A TRAVELLER
55.   TRY TO LOOK PLEASANT
56.   A FIFTH COLUMNIST
57.   LET ME BE A NUN
58.   SMASHING EYEBROWS

KEEPING THE DAD'S ARMY CULTURE ALIVE:
59. MICK WHITMAN AS CAPTAIN MAINWARING

ABOUT

S ir Winston Churchill (30 November 1874 – 24 January 1965)
Former British Prime Minister (1940 - 1945 and 1951 - 1955)

On 14 May 1940, the Government broadcast a message asking for volunteers for the Local Defence Volunteers (LDV). These men were to act as a secondary defence force. On 23 August 1940, Winston Churchill changed the name of the LDV to Home Guard.

The Home Guard was formed because of a risk of invasion from Nazi Germany and their allies. Operational from 1940 until 1944, the Home Guard, which compromised 1.5 million local volunteers, comprised men otherwise ineligible for military service.

1
Nico 2020

 EL LAWRENCE

ACTOR

Geoffrey Lumsden (26 December 1914 – 4 March 1984) as Captain Square
Series 1, episode 3: 'Command Decision'
First broadcast (BBC1): 14 August 1968

"Now, what do you see in your mind's eye when I say the word El Lawrence? El Lawrence, man, El Lawrence?"
– Captain Square

"What do you see in your mind's eye, Wilson?"
– Captain Mainwaring

"An ice cream, Sir?" – Sergeant Wilson

2
Nico
2020

YOUR FAVOURITE TOBACCO

ACTOR

Pamela Cundell (15 January 1920 – 14 February 2015) as Mrs Fox
Series 3, episode 1: 'The Armoured Might Of Lance Corporal Jones'
First broadcast (BBC1): 11 September 1969

"By the way, I bought that for you."

"Oh, what is it?" – Corporal Jones, butcher by day

"Your favourite tobacco."

"Thank you very much, Madam."

"And I'll be in later in the week." – Mrs Fox, winking

Nico 2020

CARROTS & ONIONS

ACTOR

Alan Tilvern (5 November 1918 – 17 December 2003) as Captain Rodrigues
Series 3, episode 2: 'Battle School'
First broadcast (BBC1): 18 September 1969

"Here, some carrots and onions."

"Onions..." – Sergeant Wilson

"What's wrong with onions? I always eat them."

"I'd never have guessed." – Sergeant Wilson

4
Nico
2022

# A FAG IN YOUR FOOD

ACTOR

Arthur Lowe (22 September 1915– 15 April 1982) as Captain Mainwaring
Series 3, episode 2: 'Battle School'
First broadcast (BBC1): 18 September 1969

Captain Rodrigues, supervising lunch:
"You've got only fifteen minutes. Hurry, hurry, we haven't got all night."

"You are like a lot of old women. Come on, hurry, hurry."

(Using his fingers to fish a cigarette out of Captain Mainwaring's tin)
"What did I tell you about the hygiene? Clean, clean."

5
Nico 2022

# THE VERGER

ACTOR

Edward Sinclair Perry (03 February 1914 -29 August 1977) as Maurice Yeatman, first the caretaker and from the third series onwards, the Verger of St. Aldhem's Church of Walmington-on-Sea
Set photo from series 3, episode 4: 'The Bullet Is Not For Firing'
First broadcast (BBC1): 2 October 1969

"If you ask me, most of the damage is being done by
the ones who are supposed to be on our side."

6
Nico
2020

 # THE VICAR

ACTOR

Frank Williams (2 July 1931 – 26 June 2022) as the Vicar Reverend Timothy Farthing
Series 3, episode 4: 'This Bullet Is Not For Firing'
First broadcast (BBC1): 2 October 1969

"Mr Mainwaring, if you can do your blood-curdling bayonet practice in the middle of my responses, I can do my Jubilate in the middle of your enquiry."

YOU
Nico 2020

 A LOT OF LAUGHING

ACTOR

Anthony Sagar (19 June 1920 – 24 January 1973) as the Drill Sergeant
Series 3, episode 6: 'Room At The Bottom'
First broadcast (BBC1): 16 October 1969

"What's the matter with you lot? Ain't you got no sense of humour?"

"Come on, have a good laugh, get some air in your lungs.
I do a lot of laughing, I do."

Nico 2020

VIOLET GIBBONS

ACTOR

Jenny Thomas (date unknown - 16 August 2021) as Violet Gibbons
Series 3, episode 9: 'War Dance'
First broadcast (BBC1): 6 November 1969

"When I woke up this morning, I wanted to run to the top of the church
tower and shout it to the winds, 'I love Violet Gibbons'.
I wanted to shout, but I didn't." – Frank Pike

"I think you are very wise." – Sergeant Wilsonn

Violet is Pike's girlfriend. She used to work in a fish shop. Fish and chips were not rationed during the world wars. The British Government safeguarded both the supply of fish and potatoes to ensure that the dish remained as a morale booster. Churchill referred to the dish as our 'good companion'.

Nico 2022

# MRS PROSSER

ACTOR

Eleanor Smale (dates unknown) as Mrs Prosser
Series 3, episode 9: 'War Dance'
First broadcast (BBC1): 6 November 1969

(Jones announcing guests at the ball; he is also Mrs Prosser's escort)
"Ladies and gentlemen... Mr Jones and Mrs Prosser.

Excuse me, my dear, I just got to get along. Mr Mainwaring will look
after you."

Nico 2022

 PUT THAT LIGHT OUT

ACTOR

Bill Pertwee (21 July 1926 – 27 May 2013) as Chief Warden Hodges
Set photo from series 3, episode 10: 'Menace From the Deep'
First broadcast (BBC1): 13 November 1969

"Put that light out!

Put that light out!"

ARP (Air Raid Precautions) wardens patrolled the streets during the blackout to ensure that no light was visible; lights could be spotted by German bombers. If a light was seen shining, the warden would alert people by shouting the now famous phrase "Put that light out!"

The wardens also reported the extent of bomb damage and assessed the local need for help from the emergency and rescue services. They used their knowledge of their local areas to help find and reunite families separated in the rush to find shelter from the air raids. They were issued with blue overalls, black ARP badges and helmets.

W
11
Nico 2022

 ACTUALLY, IT'S BLUE

ACTOR

M iranda Hampton (01 January 1937) as the lady with the blue…
Series 3, episode 12: 'Man Hunt'
First broadcast (BBC1): 27 November 1969

"I was just wondering if I could possibly… If you wouldn't
mind, if I…" – Sergeant Wilson

"Come on in, won't you?" The lady beckons Wilson in, adding
to the others, including Captain Mainwaring:
"Not you. Just him."

 # OLD TRICKS AGAIN

ACTOR

Leon Cortez (27 May 1898 – 31 December 1970) as the old man at the door
Series 3, episode 12: 'Man Hunt'
First broadcast (BBC1): 27 November 1969

"Beryl, up to your old tricks again, are you, eh?
I'll teach you, my girl. I'll teach you."

The platoon is trying to trace some parachute silk which Walker has had made up into ladies' knickers. The search involves knocking on doors and asking to see said knickers. This gentleman is far from pleased when they ask to see his wife's underwear.

The landmine parachute, or any parachute, was greatly sought after, as they were made of pure silk. Ladies turned them into a variety of ladies' undergarments.

13
Nico
2021

 # FUNNY TEMPERED

ACTOR

Colin Bean (15 April 1926 – 20 June 2009) as Private Sponge
Series 4, episode 1: 'The Big Parade'
First broadcast (BBC1): 25 September 1970

"As we saw a ram being used as a mascot on that parade in the newsreel, perhaps we could use a ram ourselves." – Sergeant Wilson

"Aye, Private Sponge here, he's a farmer. He maybe could help us."
– Private Fraser

"Yes, I've got a few, but they're very funny tempered at this time of the year."
– Private Sponge

14
Nico
2021

GENERALE MONTEVERDI

ACTOR

Edward Evans (4 June 1914 – 20 December 2001) as Italian Generale Franco Bruno Tello Monteverdi (Italian Prisoner of War)
Series 4, episode 5: 'Don't Fence Me In'
First broadcast (BBC1): 23 October 1970

```
"You are only a Capitano.

You should stand up for me because I am a Generale.

Si, Generale Franco Bruno Tello Monteverdi."
```

Generale Franco Bruno Tello Monteverdi is the Senior Officer in an Italian prison camp, which the platoon has been sent to guard. Under Generale Monteverdi, order in the prison camp is very lax.

From July 1941, Italian prisoners captured in the Mediterranean were brought to Britain, up to almost 100,000 Italian Prisoners of War (POWs). The Italian POWs were given considerable freedom and worked particularly in agriculture and forestry, where unskilled labour was in short supply or unavailable.

15
Nico
2022

 # ESSENTIAL SUPPLIES

ACTOR

James Beck (21 February 1929 – 6 August 1973) as Private Joe Walker Series 4, episode 7: 'Put That Light Out'
First broadcast (BBC1): 6 November 1970

"Excuse me, Sir. I won't be able to go along tonight because I'm delivering essential supplies... it's vital, it's for the nurses."

"Not elastic again, is it?" – Captain Mainwaring

"No, it's hairpins."

Walker deals on the black market, so is consequently known as a 'spiv'. The word spiv is slang for a type of petty criminal who deals in illicit, typically black market, goods. The word was particularly used during the Second World War and in the post-war period, when many goods were rationed. In wartime, when everyone was expected to 'do their bit', the activities of the spivs and their suppliers were not well received. Penalties were severe for those caught dealing, including a fine of up to £500 and a two-year prison sentence.

NICO 2021

 # NOT GIVING IN

ACTOR

Carmen Silvera (2 June 1922 – 3 August 2002) as Mrs Fiona Grey
Series 4, episode 9: 'Mum's Army'
First broadcast (BBC1): 20 November 1970

"I brought my mother down from London because of the bombing.
I'd loved to have stayed.
Not that there was very much I could've done, but just being there would
have shown that wretched little Hitler we're not going to give in."

17
Nico
2021

 # A LAAARGE BUILDING

ACTOR

Rose Hill (5 June 1914 – 22 December 2003) as Mrs Cole
Series 4, episode 12: 'Uninvited Guests'
First broadcast (BBC1): 11 December 1970

"A large building next to St. Aldhem's Church."
– Hodges, dictating to Mrs Cole

"A large... a laaaarge building... yes." – Mrs Cole

"Next to St. Aldhem's Church." – Hodges)

"Church. Mor... Mortimer Road." – Mrs Cole

"Worse than you lot, she is."
– Hodges (to Mainwaring who he is sharing an office with)

18
W
ARP
Nico 2021

 NAPOLEON

ACTOR

Arthur Lowe (22 September 1915 – 15 April 1982) as Napoleon
Series 5, episode 3: 'A Soldier's Farewell'
First broadcast (BBC1): 20 Oktober 1972

```
"Soldiers of France
Our cause is lost.

Your Emperor must say goodbye.
With this kiss, I embrace you all."
```

Nico
2022

 # MRS YEATMAN

ACTOR

Olive Mercer (15 September 1905 – 2 January 1983) as Mrs Yeatman, the verger's wife
Series 5, episode 4: 'Getting The Bird'
First broadcast (BBC1): 27 October 1972

"I didn't get any sausages."

"You wasn't at Dunkirk, was you?"
– Corporal Jones in his day job as the butcher

"No, but I made tea for them and I rolled bandages."

"You can't get sausages for that. I've got to draw the
line somewhere." – Jones

20
Nico
2020

THROUGH THE CEILING

ACTORS

James Beck (21 February 1929 – 6 August 1973) as Private Joe Walker
Wendy Richard (20 July 1943 – 26 February 2009) as Shirley
Series 5, episode 7: 'The King Was In His Counting House'
First broadcast (BBC1): 17 November 1972

"Ah, that sounds like Elizabeth coming down."
- Captain Mainwaring

"Through the ceiling." - Joe Walker

 # A PRETTY BROOCH

ACTOR

Margaret E. Don (30 November 1941) as the waitress
Series 5, episode 10: 'Brain Versus Brawn'
First broadcast (BBC1): 8 December 1972

"I say, what a pretty brooch you've got on.
It seems to match the colouring of your hair so well."
– Sergeant Wilson

"Thank you, Sir. I'll slip you another one when you've finished that."

22
Nico
2021

 # SPECIAL DUTIES

ACTOR

Michael Knowles (26 April 1937) as Captain Stewart
Series 5, episode 12: 'Round And Round Went the Great Big Wheel'
First broadcast (BBC1): 22 December 1972

"Say no more, Captain Stewart. You want us for special duties."
– Captain Mainwaring

"Special duties... Yes, that's it. I want you for special duties."

23

 # MAD, MAD, MAD

ACTOR

John Laurie (25 March 1897 – 23 June 1980) as Private Frazer
Series 5, episode 13: 'Time On My Hands'
First broadcast (BBC1): 29 December 1972

"Did you hear what I said, Captain Mainwaring? Mad... MAD... MAD."

"Stop rolling your eyes, Frazer." – Mainwaring

24
Nico
2020

 # THEM GERMANS MAKE...

ACTOR

Harold Bennett (17 November 1899 – 15 September 1981) as Mr Sidney Blewitt
Series 5, episode 13: 'Time On My Hands'
First broadcast (BBC1): 29 December 1972

"Them Germans make very good megaphones, loudspeakers, radios
and gramophones.

They make very good gramophones, them Germans."

Nico 2022

## 25

IN A HUDDLE, AT THE DOUBLE

ACTORS

James Beck (21 February 1929 – 6 August 1973) as Private Joe Walker
Emmett Hennessy (December 1946) as a crew-member of the German U-boat
Series 6, episode 1: 'The Deadly Attachment'
First broadcast (BBC1): 31 October 1973

"In a huddle, at the double, in a small group in the centre of the hall." – Corporal Jones to the German prisoners

CP
1

YOU WILL EAT SOGGY CHIPS

ACTOR

Philip Madoc (5 July 1934 – 5 March 2012) as the U-boat captain

Series 6, episode 1: 'The Deadly Attachment'
First broadcast (BBC1): 31 October 1973

"And I don't want any nasty, soggy chips.
I want mine crisp und light brown."

"If I say you will eat soggy chips, you will eat soggy chips."
– Captain Mainwaring

"Soggy chips," notes Private Walker.

 # ON ZE LIST...

ACTORS

Philip Madoc (5 July 1934 – 5 March 2012) as the U-boat captain
Arthur Lowe (22 September 1915 – 15 April 1982) as Captain Mainwaring

Series 6, episode 1: 'The Deadly Attachment'
First broadcast (BBC1): 31 October 1973

```
"Your name will also go on ze list. What is it?"

"Don't tell him, Pike." - Captain Mainwaring
```

The U-boat captain and his crew are being guarded by the platoon. The Germans attempt to get the better of the platoon. When World War II began, Germany had 57 submarines under the command of Commodore Karl Dönitz, who believed the war would be decided in the Atlantic Ocean with 300 U-boats. Germany ended up building 1162 U-boats.

 DAVID COPPERFIELD

ACTOR

Arnold Ridley (7 January 1896 – 12 March 1984) as Private Godfrey
Series 6, episode 1: 'The Deadly Attachment'
First broadcast (BBC1): 31 October 1973

"I saw Freddie Bartholomew in *David Copperfield*...
Eh... There was nothing in that."

"I've never heard such drivel in my life. David Copp..."
– Captain Mainwaring

29
Nico 2022

 # THE COLONEL

ACTOR

Robert Raglan (7 April 1909 – 18 July 1985) as the Colonel
Series 6, episode 1: 'The Deadly Attachment'
First broadcast (BBC1): 31 October 1973

"Where on earth are you taking the prisoners, Mainwaring?"

"What's the matter with you, man?
You're white as a sheet, as if you've seen a ghost."

# WHAT AM I?

ACTORS

Fulton Mackay (12 August 1922 – 6 June 1987) as Captain Ramsey
Clive Dunn (9 January 1920 – 6 November 2012) as Corporal Jones
Series 6, episode 4: 'We Know Our Onions'
First broadcast (BBC1): 21 November 1974

"When I blow my whistle, I am a Gestapo Officer.
What am I? Come on man, come on..."

"Eh... you're a Gestoffi Sapo..." – Corporal Jones

 # I HATE COWARDS

ACTORS

Fulton Mackay (12 August 1922 – 6 June 1987) as Captain Ramsey
Ian Lavender (1946) as Private Frank Pike
Series 6, episode 4: 'We Know Our Onions'
First broadcast (BBC1): 21 November 1974

"Why are you crying, laddie?" – Captain Ramsey

"I'm not crying." – Private Pike

"Yes, you are. You're a coward. I hate cowards."
– Captain Ramsey

32
HOME GUARD
NICO
2021

OUTSTANDINGLY SUITABLE

ACTOR

Eric Longworth (20 July 1918 – 20 August 2008) as Mr Gordon, the Town Clerk
Series 6, episode 5: 'The Honourable Man'
First broadcast (BBC1): 28 November 1973

"There is one man, and he is sitting here, who is outstandingly suitable
to get his teeth into this sort of do...

...and I'm going to ask him, with your approval, I'm sure, to take the
chair. Captain George Mainwaring."

33
Nico
2020

HONOUR YOUR WORKERS

ACTORS

Gabor Vernon (23 March 1925 - 23 April 1985) as Mr Vladislovski, "Well, his name is immaterial really …"
Anna Maria Pravda (29 January 1916 – 22 May 2008) as the translator
Series 6, episode 5: 'The Honourable Man'
First broadcast (BBC1): 28 November 1973

"I represent the workers of the Soviet Union. You, who are sitting here, are not workers. You have soft faces…

You are bourgeois middle clas…

You are giving me honour. You should honour your own workers!"

34
NICO 2021

 # PWINCE 439

ACTOR

Jonathan Cecil (22 February 1939 – 22 September 2011) as Captain Cadbury
Series 6, episode 6: 'Things That Go Bump In The Night'
First broadcast (BBC1): 5 December 1973

"These are only half-twained war wecwuits. Not a bad bunch weally, except
for that one, Pwince 439. He's a weal twoublemaker, upsets the others.
Yes, you, 439. Stand to attention when I'm speaking to you."

Captain Cadbury does the admin at a dog training school.

Dogs were trained by the War Office to scent mines, rescue civilians trapped under bombed buildings, act as messengers on the front lines, and track down German parachutists. Some were also chosen to assist airborne troops on D-Day but certainly not Pwince 439... he was a real twoublemaker.

# GREAT SCOTT, GRAPES!

ACTOR

Arthur Lowe (22 September 1915 – 15 April 1982) as Captain Mainwaring
Series 6, episode 7: 'The Recruit'
First broadcast (BBC1): 12 December 1973

"I've bought these for you, Sir." – Corporal Jones

"Great Scott, grapes! I haven't tasted a grape since 1939."

"Well, they're not real grapes, Sir. We impersonated them
from electric light wires, see, and shaved gooseberries."
– Corporal Jones

THE POWER OF THE PRESS

ACTOR

Talfryn Thomas (31 October 1922 – 4 November 1982) as Private Cheeseman, reporter who became WC (War Correspondent) of the Walmington-on-Sea Home Guard Platoon

Set photo, series 7, episode 2: 'Man of Action'
First broadcast (BBC1): 22 November 1974

"Captain Mainwaring. Man of action."

To Captain Mainwaring:
"I'm right behind you, boyo."

"The power of the press, remember. The power of the press!"

# HEAVILY DISGUISED

ACTOR

Clive Dunn (9 January 1920 – 6 November 2012) as Lance Corporal Jones and Jones the butcher, when not on active service.
Series 7, episode 4: 'The Godiva Affair'
First broadcast (BBC1): 6 December 1974

"Pst, pst... Mr Mainwaring.

You won't give me away, will you, Sir?

I'm heavily disguised. I don't want anyone to recognise me."

38
DAILY
DUTCH
DRAWER
ON THE
LOOSE
Nico
2020

# MES CHERS CAMARADES

ACTOR

John Hart Dyke (10 November 1929 – 2 February 2018) as the French general
Series 7, episode 5: 'The Captain's Car'
First broadcast (BBC1): 13 December 1974

"Men chers camarades d'armes
Je ne puis pas parler... Mon coeur deborde. Mais... merci."

(My dear comrades in arms
I cannot speak... My heart is overflowing. But... thank you.)

Nico
2021

 # NO KISS FOR THE VICAR

ACTOR

Frank Williams (2 July 1931 – 26 June 2022) as the vicar, Reverend Timothy Farthing
Series 7, episode 5: 'The Captain's Car'
First broadcast (BBC1): 13 December 1974

"Allons enfants de la patrie
Le jour de gloire est arrivé..."

"...there just wasn't time to learn the rest.
They are only little boys, you know."

Translation:
Come on, children of the fatherland, the day of glory has arrived.

40

 # IT'S WEDNESDAY

ACTOR

Dave Butler (1936 – 25 December 1996) as farm hand on the North Barrington Turkey Farm
Series 7, episode 6: 'Turkey Dinner'
First broadcast (BBC1): 23 December 1974

"It's Wednesday."

"Captain Mainwaring, why don't we put a dab of paint on each turkey as we count?" – Corporal Jones

"Mr Boggis wouldn't like that. He don't like people painting his turkeys."

41

 # IT MADE MEN OF US

ACTOR

John Laurie (25 March 1897 – 23 June 1980) Private Frazer
Series 7, episode 6: 'Turkey Dinner'
First broadcast (BBC1): 12 December 1973

> "My mother made gravy. It was thin and weak.
> And my father used to belt us regular as clockwork every night.
> But it made men of us."

Private Frazer comes from the Isle of Barra, a wild and lonely place. Barra is an island in the Outer Hebrides, Scotland. During W.W. II, the North-West Highlands played a vital part in the Battle of the Atlantic.

Gaelic was the primary language; many islanders didn't speak any English. Transport was limited and many locals had never even visited the mainland before being sent to their military training. The blackouts were never too much of a problem on the islands, as electricity had not been introduced.

42
Nico 2022

# I COULDN'T DO HIM, DEAR

ACTOR

Hilda Fenemore (22 April 1914 – 13 April 2004) as Queenie Beal
Series 8, episode 1: 'Ring Them Bells'
First broadcast (BBC1): 5 September 1975

"Ooh, I couldn't do him, I couldn't do him, dear.

Look at his feet, I ain't got no jackboots that size.

Tiny? He's got girls' feet."

43
Nico
2021

 **CIS INSISTS...**

ACTOR

John Bardon (25 August 1939 – 12 September 2014) as Harold Forster
Series 8, episode 1: 'Ring Them Bells'
First broadcast (BBC1): 5 September 1975

"Jack insists on being with Cis and Cis insists
on being with Jack.

Well, they're always together."

44
Nico
2022

# SCHWEINHUND...

ACTOR

Ian Lavender (1946) as Private Frank Pike
Series 8, episode 1: 'Ring Them Bells'
First broadcast (BBC1): 5 September 1975

"Schweinhund!"

"So, we are the masters now...
You have five seconds to tell us your plans, or else,
it is kaput!"

## 45

YOU LOOK LIKE AN EAGLE

ACTOR

John Laurie (25 March 1897 – 23 June 1980) as Private Frazer
Series: 8, episode 1: 'Ring them Bells'
First broadcast (BBC1): 5 September 1975

"I feel a right soppy twerp, wearing this ridiculous get-up."
-Private Frazer

"Mr Frazer, I don't think you look like a fool.

I think that helmet makes you look like an eagle."

– Private Godfrey

46

NICE BIT OF WEATHER...

ACTOR

Jack Haig (5 January 1913- 4 July 1989) as Mr Palethorpe, landlord of the Six Bells
Series 8, episode 1: 'Ring Them Bells'
First broadcast (BBC1): 5 September 1975

Mr Palethorpe is the landlord of the Six Bells, a public house. He is startled one day when Mainwaring's men call in for a drink while dressed in German uniforms. The platoon are in costume for a training film.

Pubs played an important role in wartime life. In contrast to the First World War, when drinking and the pubs were thought to be harming the war effort and were subject to major restrictions, in the Second World War, the pub was viewed as important for maintaining morale.

# GOOD MORNING, MEIN HOST

ACTOR

Ian Lavender (1946) as Private Frank Pike
Series 8, episode 1: 'Ring Them Bells'
First broadcast (BBC1): 5 September 1975

"What can I get..." – Mr Palethorpe

"Good afternoon, Mein Host. Sixteen shandies mit the ginger beer."

"Gi... gi... gi... Pints or halves?" – Mr Palethorpe

"Pints!"

ALL BOYS DO IT, YOU KNOW

ACTOR

Ian Lavender (1946) as Private Frank Pike
Series 8, episode 2: 'When You've Got To Go'
First broadcast (BBC1): 12 September 1975

```
"Why does he keep doing that face thing?"
- Captain Mainwaring
```

```
"I think it's just his age, Sir. All boys do it, you know."
- Sergeant Wilson
```

```
"I didn't." Captain Mainwaring
```

Pike is the youngest of the platoon and therefore eligible for conscription into the armed forces. He is very nervous about this.

The National Service (Armed Forces) Act imposed conscription on all males aged between 18 and 41 who had to register for service. Those medically unfit (rare blood group), working in key industries, or allergic to army rations, were exempted.

49
Nico
2020

 # NOT MY FRANK

ACTOR

Janet Davies (14 September 1927 – 22 September 1986) as Mrs Mavis Pike
Series 8, episode 2: 'When You've Got To Go'
First broadcast (BBC1): 12 September 1975

"You'll have to go and see them, Arthur.
They're not having my Frank for a soldier."

"No, I've asked to be put in the RAF." – Private Pike (looking smug))

Mrs Mavis Pike is a typical war-time housewife who has to feed her family on wartime rations. In January 1940, food rationing was introduced. Everyone was given a ration book with coupons, required to buy rationed goods.

Basic food such as sugar, meat, fats, bacon and cheese were directly rationed by coupons; some goods were rationed by a point system (for example biscuits, cereals, dried fruit). Not all food was rationed, exceptions were fish and chips, fresh fruit and vegetables.

Nico 2020

 HAPPY LAUGHING FACES

ACTOR

Clive Dunn (9 January 1920 – 6 November 2012) as Lance Corporal Jones, Jones the butcher when not on active service
Series 8, episode 3: 'Is There Honey Still For Tea?'
First broadcast (BBC1): 19 September 1975

"...He is our commanding officer and a gentleman. And furthermore...

Just a minute...

Those plaster pigs have not got comic expressions on their faces,
they've got happy, laughing faces."

51
Nico 2022

 # MERELY THE SERVANT

ACTOR

Arthur Lowe (22 September 1915 – 15 April 1982), Captain Mainwaring of the Home Guard, the Walmington-on-Sea bank manager in his daily life.

Series 8, episode 5: 'High Finance'
First broadcast (BBC1): 3 October 1975

"I am merely the servant of the bank, to carry out the policy of the bank.
Isn't that so, Wilson?"

"That is so, Sir. Yes, merely the servant." – Sergeant Wilson1son

52
Nico 2022

 YOUR COLLEAGUE?

ACTOR

Gabor Vernon (23 March 1925- 23 April 1985) as the Polish Army officer
Series 8, episode 6: 'The Face On The Poster'
First broadcast (BBC1): 10 October 1975

"I demand the release of my colleague." – Captain Mainwaring

"Ah, so that man is your colleague, eh? That's very interesting."

Because of a mix-up with a photograph on a wanted poster, the Polish officer has arrested Corporal Jones.

The Free Polish forces, in Britain, made substantial contributions to the allied war effort, fighting in the air, on land and at sea. Polish pilots joined the RAF, Polish land forces fought in Italy (Monte Cassino), the Polish Airborne brigade fought at Arnhem, and the Polish navy took part in D-Day. Also, the Polish intelligence service provided invaluable information to Allied Intelligence by giving them a Polish-made copy of the so-called Enigma code machine, crucial to the deciphering of the German radio messages.

T
53
DAN
NOTIFY
POLI
Nico 2020

# I'M A TRAVELLER

ACTOR

Arthur Lowe (22 September – 15 April 1982) as Barry Mainwaring, Captain George Mainwaring's brother (double role) Series 8, episode 7 (second Christmas special): 'My Brother And I'
First broadcast (BBC1): 26 December 1975

"I'm a traveller. Guess what I'm travelling in?"

"Oh, man, I have no idea." – Private Frazer

"You've got it: jokes, carnival novelties."

Nico 2021

## 54

TRY TO LOOK PLEASANT

ACTOR

John Le Mesurier (5 December 1912 – 15 November 1983) as Sergeant Wilson
Series 8, episode 7: 'My Brother And I'
First broadcast (BBC1): 26 December 1975

"What would you like me to do, Sir?"

"Oh, eh... Just try to look pleasant." – Captain Mainwaring

"I think Sergeant Wilson ought to play some light music on the
piano. That's pleasant." – Corporal Jones

"All right, you can play the piano, Wilson, but not very loudly."
– Captain Mainwaringg

55
Nico 2020

# A FIFTH COLUMNIST

ACTOR

Arthur Lowe (22 September 1915 – 15 April 1982) as Captain Mainwaring
Series 9, episode 1: 'Wake Up Walmington'
First broadcast (BBC1): 2 October 1977

"Does this fit the bill, Sir?" – Sergeant Wilson

"I don't think I have ever seen anything look so stupid in my life."

"Not so stupid as wearing an eye patch with glasses."
– Sergeant Wilson

Nico
2020

 LET ME BE A NUN

ACTOR

Clive Dunn (9 January 1920 – 6 November 2012) as Lance Corporal Jones
Series 9, episode 1: 'Wake Up Walmington'
First broadcast (BBC1): 2 October 1977

"Bet you didn't know it was me, Sir?"

"You've gone too far now." – Captain Mainwaring

"Let me be a nun, Captain Mainwaring.
Everyone's dressing up as nuns these days. It's all in the papers."

57
Nico 2020

SMASHING EYEBROWS

ACTOR

Jean Gilpin (1950) as Sylvia Hodges (ARP Warden Hodges' niece)
Series 9, episode 2: 'The Making Of Private Pike'
First broadcast (BBC1): 9 October 1977

"You've got smashing eyebrows."

"Have I?" – Private Pike

"They're like Tyrone Power."

Sylvia, ARP Warden Hodges' niece, meets Frank Pike when she is visiting her uncle in Walmington-on-Sea.
Sylvia is in Auxiliary Territorial Service (ATS), formed in 1938, tasking women with a range of vital roles during the war, starting as cooks, clerks, orderlies, storekeepers and drivers but the jobs available were gradually broadened to technical jobs as demand for personnel increased.

By 1943, about 56,000 women were even serving with anti-aircraft guns. At 19, Princess Elizabeth joined the Auxiliary Territorial Service. She trained as a driver and mechanic. Around 250,000 women served in the ATS.

58
Nico 2020

MICK WHITMAN
AS CAPTAIN MAINWARING

ABOUT

Mick Whitman (12 September 1942) re-enactment as Captain Mainwaring in Thetford, Norfolk, since 2010.

Mick Whitman (1942), the re-enactment Captain of the Home Guard Platoon in Thetford (Norfolk) for over 14 years now, is leading the platoon in a way the good Captain can be proud of.

Loved by his men, loved by his wife. Yes, there are differences, but no Dad's Army book would be complete without a picture of this great leader who is always in for some fun, such as the Dutch medal ceremony at the Captain Mainwaring statue in Thetford in 2018.

Mick Whitman and his men were very pleased with it. Standing to attention, standing in the shoes of Captain Mainwaring and the platoon, Mick Whitman received a medal from Dutch Dad's Army fans. It was their tribute to the culture, the history and the joy that this marvellous British comedy gives us all. Keeping the Dad's Army culture alive; without the re-enactment platoon of Mick Whitman and his men, it's almost impossible.

59
Nico 2022

# FROM THE DUTCH DRAWER

At the beginning of the first lockdown period in 2020, a friend invited me to join online drawing lessons, given by a sympathetic artist in Chelmsford, five days a week for several months. It was a unique opportunity to follow these lessons from the Netherlands. When they ended, I began to draw the characters from my favourite British sitcom, *Dad's Army*.

I have always been a great fan of *Dad's Army* since 1972, when it was first broadcasted in the Netherlands. A wonderful sitcom about the British Home Guard which today still has many fans on this side of the North Sea.

With just under 60 drawings, the question arose: what to do with them? The thought came up to publish them with the typical quotes and catchphrases of the characters and, in some cases, provide some historical background.

I hope you enjoy the drawings as much as I enjoyed creating them.

Nico Broekhuis

# ACKNOWLEDGEMENTS

An idea became a project for which I got a lot of help, so it is time now to say a word of thanks to:

James Wilkinson from Paintpop.com for all his drawing lessons during lockdown. Lindsey Brannon for drawing me into the James Wilkinson drawing club without whom I would probably never have drawn again.

WWT Ltd and JPP Ltd for their kind permission to use the original Dad's Army quotes and catch phrases. The BBC for their permission to use the original photos as a basis for the drawings.

Wim Poppelaars for having a critical eye on the drawings, and proofreading.

Susan O'Neil for writing the historical background information and editing.

And my son, Erik Broekhuis, for all the hours he dedicated to his great design.

Thank you all.

 ABOUT CITY STONE PUBLISHING

**INDIE PUBLISHER WITH A PASSION FOR THE WRITTEN WORD
AND A HEART THAT BEATS FOR OUR AUTHORS**

We are an imaginative and enthusiastic traditional publisher.

Our ambition is two-fold:
To develop outstanding books and works alongside our authors
To be a beacon of advice and a provider of services for indie authors

We are not just about the books; we build relationships with our authors. Because we both write, we know what (indie) authors want. That is how we work: in cooperation and partnership with our authors.

From dark and gritty crime and psychological thrillers, adventurous fantasy, entertaining women's fiction, and intriguing contemporary novels to interesting and insightful non-fiction and visionary poetry, we publish it all.

Visit our website: www.citystonepublishing.com